Marked By The Nyx Breaker

A Spicy Ticking Clock Fated Mates Romance

VA Browning

Contents

About the author

V.A. Browning writes contemporary romance that sizzles with workplace tension and authentic emotional depth. Her passion for storytelling was born from years of being a voracious reader who devoured romance novels by the stack, always searching for stories that balanced smart, capable characters with the messy, wonderful reality of falling in love. After spending over a decade in the hospitality industry, she discovered that the high-pressure, fast-paced world of hotels and restaurants provided the perfect backdrop for the kind of intense, slow-burn romance she loves to read—and write.

Her novels draw directly from her professional experience, bringing insider knowledge to stories about driven characters who find love in the most unexpected places. V.A. specializes in workplace romance featuring competent, passionate people who are masters of their professional domains but complete disasters when it comes to matters of the heart. She believes the best love stories happen when two people let their carefully constructed armor crack just enough to let someone else in, and she's particularly drawn to exploring how cultural heritage and family legacy shape the way we love.

When she's not crafting the perfect enemies-to-lovers dynamic or perfecting a hero's swoon-worthy declaration scene, V.A. can be found in her cozy home office overlooking her garden, usually with a diet coke within arm's reach and her two rescue dogs—a mischievous Whippet named Louie and a silly Boxer named Rocky—sprawled at her feet. Her ideal Sunday involves farmers market visits for fresh flowers and artisanal coffee, followed by afternoon sewing sessions where she creates quilts from vintage fabrics she's collected over the years. She's a firm believer that the best stories, like the best meals, are meant to be savored slowly.

V.A. is passionate about representing authentic cultural experiences in her work. She lives in Oklahoma with her two dogs, an ever-growing collection of fabric scraps, and enough romance novels to stock a small bookstore. She's currently working on her next novel, another workplace romance that promises to deliver the same blend of professional competence, cultural richness, and irresistible romantic tension that readers expect from her stories. When readers ask her about her writing philosophy, she always says the same thing: every reader deserves a happily-ever-after that feels both swoon-worthy and real, featuring characters who are passionate, flawed, and deeply, beautifully human.

Learn about all the books she has available at www.nickannypublishing.com/va-browning/

Read More here: books.vabrowing.com

Chapter 1: The Curse Engine

Cassius stared at the reinforced stone wall of the Council safe house and tried giving it his most intimidating, centuries-old warrior glare.

The wall remained entirely unbothered.

He shifted his weight on the uncomfortable, overly modern sofa, feeling a distinct chill seep through his clothes. Cassius tried to summon the appropriate amount of brooding. He was mostly just cold, and his lower back ached from sleeping on a mattress apparently made of rigid principle.

More pressing than the cold, however, was the burning.

The curse marks, spidery ink-black veins, slithered beneath the skin of his forearms, pulsing with a rhythm that told him his time was almost up. Six months of total isolation. Six months of his shadows rotting from the inside out thanks to a dying witch's petty, dramatic revenge. Six months where any physical contact with a living thing resulted in immediate, explosive agony.

Except for last night.

Cassius looked down at his right hand, slowly flexing his long fingers. He replayed the moment over and over in his exceptionally bored mind. Rowan Ashford. The human curse-breaker. When her bare fingers had brushed against his wrist at Sloane Caffrey's home last night, the first deliberate contact anyone had attempted in six months, he'd braced himself for the familiar white-hot pain.

Instead, it hadn't burned. Something had happened, startling and unwelcome, and he had been turning it over since. He was a weapon, the Nyx Breaker, a commander of shadows. He did not do *warmth.* He especially didn't know how to handle the sudden, complete inability to stop thinking about holding someone's hand.

The heavy iron door of the safe house groaned open, interrupting his minor existential crisis. Cyprian Valen, the Council's resident medical expert and chief purveyor of bad news, swept into the room. He was carrying a sleek silver briefcase and looking at Cassius with the sort of detached pity usually reserved for an expensive appliance that had finally stopped working.

"You look terrible," Cyprian noted, setting his case on the metal table.

"I've been marinating in a magical problem for six months in a basement," Cassius replied, his voice a dry rasp. "They don't exactly provide exfoliating scrubs."

Cyprian snapped on a pair of latex gloves and gestured for Cassius to offer his arm. Cassius dutifully rolled up his sleeve. Cyprian hovered a glowing amethyst crystal over the black veins and watched it sputter out.

Cyprian sighed, dropping the crystal back into his case. "Well, the good news is that the progress is holding steady. The bad news is that 'steady' implies a very consistent march toward your heart. I'm afraid the Council's previous estimate was slightly optimistic. You have seven days, Cassius."

Cassius didn't blink. "Seven days until the curse consumes my shadow source completely?"

"Seven days until it becomes a distinctly permanent, highly terminal complication," Cyprian corrected. He adjusted his glasses, looking remarkably uncomfortable for a vampire who usually enjoyed being right. "The Council has authorized me to offer you the... alternative. A clean end. Dignity, rather than letting the witch's magic rot you from the inside out."

Cassius stood up, towering over the doctor. He let his shadows gather at his heels. "I am a warrior of House Nyx. I do not surrender to a witch's rant. I will wait."

"Waiting implies you have a solution coming," Cyprian pointed out sensibly.

Before Cassius could formulate a suitably dramatic reply, the heavy door slammed open again.

Rowan Ashford marched into the room, hauling a canvas duffel bag that looked like it weighed half as much as she did. She dropped the bag onto the concrete floor with a resounding *thud*, pulled a travel mug of coffee from her oversized coat pocket, and looked around the bleak safe house with deep, undeniable distaste.

"Are we paying for this aesthetic, or does the Council just naturally gravitate toward 'serial killer chic'?" she asked, taking a long drink of her coffee.

Cassius stared at her. She was entirely too awake for this hour. She wore practical black combat boots, dark jeans, and a thick sweater, her hair pulled back into a messy knot that suggested she'd spent the morning wrestling with ancient grimoires rather than a hairbrush. She looked entirely human, deeply exasperated, and smelled of vanilla and ozone.

Cassius suddenly felt acutely aware of his posture. He crossed his arms, trying to look imposing, then immediately uncrossed them because the curse flared with sharp pain. He settled for awkwardly clasping his hands behind his back.

"Miss Ashford," Cyprian greeted, sounding relieved that there was suddenly another target in the room. "I was just informing our patient of his timeline."

"Seven days," Rowan said, barely glancing at Cassius as she unzipped her duffel bag. She began pulling out silver bowls, bundles of dried herbs, and an alarming number of sharp iron tools. "Yes, Sloane filled me in. It's a very tight schedule, which means we don't have time for Council posturing."

She finally looked up, her gaze pinning Cassius in place. "Here is the plan. Today is full curse analysis. I need to map the exact magical frequency of the witch's intent. To do that, I need sustained close proximity, and I need to establish a physical anchor point. Which means I'm going to have to touch the curse marks directly for an extended period of time."

Cassius felt a spike of genuine panic that had nothing to do with terminal complications. "You cannot touch me."

Rowan sighed, rubbing her temples as if he were a particularly slow student. "I'm a curse-breaker, Cassius. Touching cursed things is literally in the job description. Do you think I break hexes via email?"

"My touch destroys everything," Cassius stated, pitching his voice into its lowest, most commanding register. He needed her to understand the danger. He needed to be intimidating.

He looked around the barren room for a demonstration prop. His eyes landed on a sad, wilting fern that someone had inexplicably left in the corner of this dungeon. Cassius stepped over to it, removed his black leather glove with a sharp, aggressive tug, and pressed a single finger to one of the drooping green leaves.

The plant shriveled, turned black, and dissolved into ash.

Cassius turned back to Rowan.

Rowan stared at the ash pile, then took another sip of her coffee. "You owe the Council thirty dollars for that fern."

Cassius blinked. "It was a demonstration of my lethal nature."

"It was dramatic vandalism," Rowan countered. "Put the glove back on and come sit at the table. I have a schedule, and we are currently four minutes behind."

Cassius felt completely unmoored. Vampires trembled when he spoke, enemies fled when he summoned his shadows, and this woman was treating him like a scheduling conflict.

He needed her to leave. He couldn't risk last night's anomaly being a fluke. If he burned her, if the curse transferred to her, the mere thought made his chest correspondingly tight.

Cassius closed the distance between them in a blur of preternatural speed. He stopped inches from her, letting his eyes bleed into the terrifying, glowing violet of his Nyx heritage. He leaned down, capturing her gaze, channeling a massive surge of vampiric compulsion into his voice.

"*You will pack your bags*," he commanded. "*You will leave this safe house, and you will not return. It is deeply inconvenient for you to be here.*"

Rowan stared back into his glowing purple eyes. She didn't blink. She didn't glaze over. Instead, her eyebrows drew together in profound irritation.

"Did you really just try to Jedi mind trick me?" she asked.

Cassius frowned, dropping the compulsion. He stared at her, thoroughly confused. "That... should have worked. Humans cannot resist a direct compulsion from a House Nyx elite."

From the corner of the room, Cyprian let out a soft, choked noise. The doctor had dropped his pen. He was staring at the two of them with wide, horrified eyes.

"She didn't even flinch," Cyprian whispered. "Total immunity to direct compulsion."

Cassius froze. The ancient texts. The old campfire stories. Total immunity to compulsion from a specific vampire was the absolute biological marker of only one phenomenon.

He looked back at Rowan. Her pulse was at her throat. She was still standing there, still annoyed, which was somehow the most impossible part.

"That confirms it," Cyprian breathed, backing up slightly as if the two of them were about to explode. "Shadow Twin."

Rowan froze, her coffee cup abruptly halting halfway to her mouth. She looked between the two vampires. "No. Absolutely not. That's a myth. A bedtime story for overly dramatic vampire fledglings. You are not diagnosing me with a mythical soulmate condition."

Cassius felt the floor tilt beneath him. Shadow Twin. Fated mates. The universe's cosmic joke, chaining his immortal soul to a sarcastic human who worried about the cost of a fern.

"The immunity proves it's not simply a myth," Cassius said. He suddenly felt very exposed. He looked at his gloved hand, then slowly pulled the leather off. "You know exactly what it implies. It means we belong to each other."

Rowan stared at him, her denial cementing into defiance. "I'm sorry, did you really just try to claim ownership of me in a damp basement?"

"It is a biological imperative," Cassius rushed to explain, realizing how terrible it sounded. He was supposed to be a commander, not a blushing idiot. "Our souls recognize each other. It is the only reason my compulsion failed."

Rowan held up a hand. "Okay, let's pause the paranormal romance novel for a second. We have a curse to break, and I don't care if the universe thinks we should be making matching holiday cards. Put your hand on the table."

Cassius hesitated. "If my theory is correct, touching me won't hurt you because the bond protects you. But if I am wrong, the curse will strike you."

"A risk I'm willing to take because I am a professional," Rowan said sharply. She set down her coffee cup and rolled up her right sleeve. "Remove the glove. Let me do my job."

Cassius looked at her bare arm, pale and vulnerable. Slowly, he placed his bare right hand flat on the cold metal table. "Touch me."

Rowan sighed heavily. "You make the simplest requests sound like threats."

She reached out. Cassius braced himself, his jaw clenched so tightly it ached.

Rowan pressed her palm against the back of his hand.

For one heartbeat, it was nothing like pain. It ran up his arm and kept going. Rowan pulled in a sharp breath. Her hand was still in his.

Then, the curse woke up.

The black veins on Cassius's arm surged violently toward the point of contact. The witch's magic, recognizing a threat, lashed out. The warmth snapped into sharp, tearing discomfort.

Cassius shouted, trying to pull his hand away, but the magic locked them together. A jolt of dark energy arced from his skin directly into Rowan's palm.

Rowan gave a short, sharp yelp of pain, her knees buckling. The magical backlash forcefully threw them apart. Cassius hit the cement wall; Rowan stumbled backward into the table.

"Rowan!" Cassius scrambled forward.

She was clutching her right hand to her chest, breathing hard. Slowly, shaking, she lowered her hand.

Cassius stared in absolute dismay. Spreading across the back of Rowan's pale hand, reaching up past her wrist like creeping ivy, were the unmistakable, ink-black veins of the witch's curse.

Cassius dropped to his knees, his hands hovering inches from hers, terrified to touch her again. "What have I done?" he whispered, his voice cracking. "I infected you."

Rowan stared at her hand, tracing one of the black veins with her thumb. She looked up at Cassius, then over to

Cyprian, who was leaning against the far wall looking like he badly needed a drink.

"Well," Rowan said, her voice remarkably level for someone who had just been handed a magical death sentence. She let out a long, slow breath. "I'd really like to file a complaint about this soulmate situation."

Cyprian adjusted his glasses. "The curse recognized the Shadow Twin bond. It didn't just burn you, Miss Ashford. It transferred. You both have a massive problem."

Rowan looked down at her cursed hand, then back up at Cassius kneeling on the floor in front of her. She closed her eyes.

"This," she muttered, "is deeply inconvenient for my long-term life plans."

Chapter 2: Bound by Blood

Rowan Ashford stared at the back of her right hand, watching the ink-black veins, identical to the ones slithering beneath Cassius's skin, pulse with a slow, toxic rhythm.

The pain wasn't a sharp sting. It was a heavy, necrotic ache, settling deep into her marrow. She flexed her fingers, wincing as the skin pulled tight over the dark, sprawling marks that climbed past her knuckles and curled menacingly around her wrist.

"This," Rowan announced to the damp, miserable basement, her voice echoing sharply off the bare concrete, "is completely unacceptable. I don't have time to be cursed this week."

Cyprian Valen didn't disagree. He hovered his glowing amethyst crystal over her skin, his brow furrowed behind his wire-rimmed glasses. The crystal spat gray sparks against the dark magic and went dim. He looked like an IT administrator who had just discovered someone had clicked every phishing link in the company inbox.

"The magic has fully bonded to your arcane signature," Cyprian diagnosed briskly, adjusting his glasses. He tapped a silver stylus against the darkest black vein on her wrist, and Rowan hissed as cold electricity shot up her arm. "Sorry. The infection rate is identical to Cassius's. Aggressive, predatory, and stubborn. Given its current velocity, you have seven days, Miss Ashford."

Rowan dragged her free hand down her face, barely suppressing a groan. Seven days. She squeezed her eyes shut. She had a mountain of post-action paperwork waiting for her in London. She had an expired car registration that would result in a massive fine by Tuesday. She had a dentist appointment she had already rescheduled twice.

And now she was quite literally dying of a vindictive witch's rotting hex. In an underground Council safe house that smelled faintly of ozone, old dust, and unromantic bleach.

"Seven days," Rowan repeated, opening her eyes and glaring at the ceiling. "Do you know how hard it is to get a refund on a non-refundable European flight? Because I do. The Council is reimbursing me for every single penny."

She glanced sideways. Cassius, the fearsome, centuries-old Nyx Breaker, was currently huddled on the distinctly uncomfortable modern sofa. He was a terrifying entity of primordial darkness, capable of summoning blades of pure shadow... but right now, he looked like a very large, very deadly dog that had just knocked over a priceless antique vase and was waiting to be scolded.

"I have doomed you," he said.

"Oh, stop being so dramatic," Rowan snapped, yanking her hand away from Cyprian and grabbing her travel mug. It was lukewarm now, adding petty insult to profound injury. "You didn't doom me. The universe is just experiencing a severe glitch and decided to make it my problem. Cyprian, give me a solution. The Council doesn't pay me nearly enough to die on the job, and I categorically refuse to spend my last week on earth listening to him brood."

Cyprian snapped his briefcase shut with a definitive *click*. "It isn't a glitch. The witch's magic feeds on absolute isolation. It violently rejects any living intruder. You bypassed that rejection because..."

"Don't," Rowan warned, pointing her lukewarm coffee at him. "Do not say the words."

"Because you are his Shadow Twin," Cyprian stated, entirely unbothered by the threat of caffeine-based assault. He smoothed his lapels. "As I attempted to explain before you touched him, you are fated mates. Your souls recognize each other as a single unit. Therefore, the curse couldn't reject you. Instead, it established a secondary foothold."

Rowan rolled her eyes, leaning back against the cold concrete. "Right. Fated mates. Because nothing screams 'cosmic destiny' quite like being biologically tied to an emotionally stunted commander who communicates exclusively in booming threats. It's a myth, Cyprian. It's bad Victorian poetry designed to keep younger vampires entertained."

Cassius stood up, his massive frame looming awkwardly in the small space. He crossed his arms over his broad chest, instantly realized it made him look improperly aggressive, and hurriedly shoved his hands deep into his pockets. He looked entirely out of his depth.

"The lore isn't just poetry, Rowan," Cassius said, his voice dropping into a low, gravelly rasp. "Before the first Houses were even built, there was Nyx. She carved us out of the primordial night—the original Nightshades born of cold stars and ancient shadows. She made us formidable, but she also knew that a warrior without a reason to return is just a stray blade. The Shadow Twin bond was her way of giving us a home."

Rowan leaned against the concrete wall, her brow furrowed.

"She was into tactical integrity," Cassius said. "Nyx wrote the immunity into our very blood as a sovereign override. It ensures that no vampire can ever strip their mate of their will. It's an enforced equality. A partner who is forced into obedience is a weakness in the line—someone who can be exploited or broken. But a mate who stands beside you of their own choosing, who knows your strengths and weaknesses? That is a weapon no enemy can touch."

"Great. I'm a tactical asset," Rowan muttered, glancing at the black veins on her wrist. "An extremely inconvenient, highly cursed asset."

"It is your only hope of survival," Cyprian broke in practically. "The curse was designed to feed on isolation. Your Shadow Twin bond thrives on the exact opposite: connection. To outpace the witch's magic, you must strengthen the bond. The frequency of a true mate union is the only force capable of burning the hex out of your veins."

Rowan narrowed her eyes. "Explain. Fast."

"You must initiate a ritual claiming," Cyprian said, as if prescribing a course of mild antibiotics. "Physical and magical intimacy. Sustained contact, emotional vulnerability. Overwhelm the curse with connection until the magic starves."

Cassius and Rowan both looked at him.

"Complete physical union," Cyprian added, in the tone of a man who had been bracing for this part.

The silence stretched.

Cassius looked genuinely, visibly horrified. He took a substantial step back, his boots scuffing the concrete. "No."

Rowan looked at him, feeling a sudden, completely irrational prickle of offense. "Wow. Okay. Good to know I'm that repulsive."

"That is not what I meant," Cassius said quickly, his violet eyes wide and panicked. "You are human. You are fragile. I will not force you into intimacy to save my own life. I am a warrior of the House of Nyx. I face my death with honor, not by coercing a captive into my bed."

He sounded so noble, so entrenched in his tragic warrior persona, that Rowan actually laughed, sharp and slightly hysterical.

"Cassius, try to keep up," Rowan said, setting her mug down with a solid thud. "I'm already cursed. Remember? Black marks? Aching doom? I am dying in seven days too. This isn't you being a tragic hero, this is a group project. And right now, you're trying to fail us both out of a misplaced, archaic sense of chivalry."

"I cannot ask this of you"

"You're not asking," Rowan interrupted sharply. "I'm choosing. I am choosing to do this because you are highly annoying and this entire situation is a disaster, but I absolutely refuse to let a dead witch win just because you want to be a martyr. We break this curse, or I am haunting you specifically for the rest of eternity. I will float in your periphery at all times, loudly critiquing your combat stances."

Cassius stared at her. His jaw clenched. He was used to commanding armies, to soldiers trembling in his shadow.

He wasn't used to a human woman weaponizing his noble sacrifice into a logistical inconvenience. Slowly, helplessly, the fight drained out of him. He nodded. "Very well."

"Excellent," Cyprian declared, ignoring the chaotic tension. He checked his immaculate watch. "Start small. Skin-to-skin touch. Try to channel warmth into the connection without letting the pain overwhelm you. I will return tomorrow morning. Good luck."

The doctor swept out, the heavy iron door slamming shut with the dreadful finality of a prison vault.

Rowan stared at the door. Then she turned slowly to look at Cassius.

Cassius stared back at her.

They remained totally motionless for a full minute, the silence pulling tight.

"So," Rowan said eventually, clearing her throat. "Do we... draw a circle? Or just..."

"I do not know," Cassius admitted, his tone rigid. "I have never engaged in a ritual claiming. My knowledge is purely theoretical."

"Great. Beginners. That bodes perfectly for our survival." Rowan aggressively rubbed her hands together to simulate competence, kicking an empty box out of the way. "Okay. Come here. Let's start with holding hands. And trying not to pass out."

Cassius approached as if she were an unexploded bomb. He stood rigidly in front of her, his hands hovering awkwardly at his sides.

"Give me your hand," she prompted.

He slowly extended his right hand, the black veins a twisted mirror of her own. Rowan took a deep breath, braced herself, and grabbed his hand.

Instantly, a white-hot, agonizing burn flared up their arms. It felt exactly like grabbing a live wire. Rowan gritted her teeth, a sharp gasp escaping her lips as the curse fought back. Cassius visibly flinched, his jaw locking so tightly the bones popped, and attempted to pull away.

"Don't let go!" Rowan ordered, her voice squeezed through her teeth. She dug her fingernails into his knuckles.

Beneath the jagged spikes of pain, something else pushed back. Faint. Warm. Centered exactly where their palms met. His glowing violet eyes widened as he focused on the point of contact.

"You feel that?" she ground out, sweat beading on her forehead.

"Yes," he whispered roughly.

"Push on it. Think about... sunny beaches. Excellent pastries. Not murder."

"I am a weapon," Cassius grunted, "I do not think about pastries." But he closed his eyes, his brow furrowing in intense concentration. "I am focusing on the light."

They stood there for what felt like an hour but was probably only five minutes. Two capable adults standing in a dingy bunker, holding hands with their eyes squeezed shut like nervous teenagers. The heat of the connection warred violently against the agonizing chill. It was grueling in the specific way that required everything and offered nothing back.

Eventually, her trembling legs gave out.

"Break," she gasped, ripping her hand away and stumbling back against the metal table.

Cassius swayed on his feet, looking completely drained. He grabbed the back of the sofa, chest heaving. Rowan checked her hand.

"It moved," she said. Something that was almost hope.

Cassius snapped his head up, walking over quickly to peer down at her hand. The tips of the creeping black ivy on her knuckles had receded. Maybe an inch.

"It retreated," Cassius agreed, his voice echoing actual wonder. He checked his own hand. "The bond overpowered the hex."

A heavy silence fell as the adrenaline faded, leaving cold reality. They both did the math simultaneously.

An inch of retreat. Five minutes of excruciating contact. The veins traveled up past their wrists, wrapping into their forearms and heading straight for their hearts.

Rowan dropped her head onto her hands, groaning.

"Our current velocity is entirely insufficient to prevent terminal failure," Cassius said.

"Velocity?" Rowan muttered against the table. "Who talks like that?"

He ignored the critique, his expression shifting from wonder to severe strategic concern. He surveyed the sparse room, hesitating as his gaze landed on the single piece of furniture that wasn't a sofa or a table. He rubbed the back of his neck in a deeply uncharacteristic display of nervous human energy.

"We require faster escalation," he announced formally. "Cyprian stated the therapeutic effects thrive on proximity. It... it would be most tactical if we maximized our exposure."

Rowan lifted her head slowly. "Meaning?"

Cassius refused to meet her eyes, choosing instead to stare intensely at a water stain. "Meaning, for the remainder of our time here, we should share the same room for all activities. Including resting."

He paused, struggling visibly to frame the terrifying request in a way that sounded entirely un-romantic. "I am suggesting we share the bed. Purely for the curse. Assisting the bond by maintaining close physical proximity throughout our resting cycle. Not for... any other purpose."

Rowan stared at him. The terrifying, legendary Nyx Breaker was blushing.

She looked at the terribly uncomfortable-looking queen-sized bed in the corner. It suddenly looked very, very small. Then she looked back at the horrific black magic waiting to kill her.

"Fine," Rowan said, refusing to acknowledge the sudden, stupid flutter in her stomach. "But if you snore, I might actually let the witch win."

Chapter 3: Skin and Shadows

Surviving eight hours on the left side of a modern queen-sized mattress alongside a sleeping human woman was rapidly proving to be the most agonizing trial of his immortal existence.

He had not moved a single muscle since they had laid down the previous night. He was lying flat on his back, his arms pinned stiffly to his sides, staring up at the cracked, water-stained ceiling of the Council safe house. Every instinct demanded he roll over, spread out, or at the very least, reposition his stiff neck. But Rowan was asleep barely six inches away from him, her steady, rhythmic breathing the only sound in the room.

If he moved, he risked waking her. If he reached out and accidentally touched her outside of a controlled, mentally fortified ritual space, the curse would strike, sending them both spiraling into agony. So Cassius remained as rigid as a marble effigy upon a tomb, silently enduring the profound numbness spreading through his left leg.

Beside him, Rowan shifted, letting out a soft, sleepy murmur. She rolled over, throwing one arm over her head. The thick blankets pooled around her waist.

Cassius felt his jaw tighten. He kept his eyes strictly trained on the ceiling, fighting the urge to turn his head and look at her. It was entirely unacceptable for a commander to behave like a gawking fledgling. He was here for a strategic, tactical purpose. He was here to ensure the Shadow Twin bond suppressed the death hex. That was all.

"Stop breathing so loudly," Rowan mumbled, her voice thick with sleep.

Cassius blinked. "I do not require breath. I am attempting to simulate a normal human resting pattern so as not to unsettle you."

Rowan cracked one eye open, peering at him in the gray morning. "You look like you're practicing for your own funeral, Cassius. Relax. You're allowed to bend your knees."

"I am perfectly comfortable," he lied, his left leg entirely dead.

Rowan sighed, sitting up and rubbing her face. Her hair was a tangled, chaotic nest that Cassius found deeply, irrationally fascinating. She swung her legs over the edge of the bed and instinctively looked down at her right hand.

Cassius sat up instantly, his honed warrior reflexes kicking in. He looked at her hand, and the phantom heart in his chest plummeted.

The black veins were back.

Yesterday, they had fought through excruciating pain to force the hex to retreat a single inch. It had been a small, pathetic victory, but a victory nonetheless. Now, the sprawling, jagged ink had clawed its way back over her knuckles, reclaiming every inch of the territory it had lost. The curse had regenerated perfectly overnight.

Cassius stared at the dark marks scarring her pale skin. The shadows in the corners of the room thickened without his permission.

"The hex regenerated," Cassius said. "I miscalculated."

He waited.

Instead, Rowan let out a long, heavy, profoundly irritated sigh.

"I am going to leave a terrible review for this magic system," she announced, glaring at her hand. "One out of five stars. Absolutely terrible retention rate."

Cassius blinked, looking up at her. "You are... not weeping."

"Crying isn't going to fix my hand, Cassius," Rowan said, pushing herself off the bed and marching toward the small kitchenette in the corner of the room. "And neither is your tragic, brooding monologue. It means we didn't push hard enough. It means the curse regenerates when we sleep, which means we have to outpace its healing factor. Which we will figure out immediately after I have caffeine."

Cassius watched her open the small cabinet, completely at a loss. He had led armies. He had decapitated rebel warlords. Yet he was continually defeated by the pragmatic resilience of this human woman. She treated her impending, gruesome supernatural demise like a mismanaged spreadsheet.

"There was coffee left on the counter," Cassius offered, trying to be helpful in the face of her bizarre composure. "From yesterday."

Rowan slowly turned her head to look at him. Her expression was utterly flat. "Cassius, if you honestly believe I am going to drink day-old, room-temperature basement coffee while I am actively cursed, you have fundamentally misunderstood me as a person."

She pulled a small, sleek black pod from her bag and held it up. "There is a single-serve brewing machine on that counter. Make yourself useful. Make me a new cup."

Cassius stood up, rolling his shoulders to alleviate the stiffness. He walked over to the counter and stared at the machine. It was a compact, rounded piece of plastic with a water reservoir on the back and several flashing blue buttons on the top.

He stared at it in profound silence. He tapped the top lid experimentally. Nothing happened. He pressed a button containing an icon of a slightly larger cup. The machine let out an angry beep and flashed a red light at him.

After thirty seconds of intense, deeply unhelpful surveillance, Rowan crossed her arms. "Is there a problem?"

"It is... attempting to communicate with me via flashing lights," Cassius stated, his voice carefully neutral. He did not want to admit defeat to a hostile plastic box. "I believe it requires an offering."

"It's a Keurig," Rowan said, her voice dropping into the inflection of a disappointed teacher. "It requires water. Have you never made coffee before?"

Cassius drew himself up to his full, imposing height. "I have consumed the blood of my enemies. I have survived on the bitter herbs of the northern highlands during the long wars. I do not typically operate... small, flashing appliances that beep at me aggressively."

Rowan closed her eyes, pinching the bridge of her nose. "Right. Okay. The immortal, legendary Nyx Breaker is defeated by a kitchen appliance. This is going in my memoirs. Move over."

She stepped up beside him, ignoring the way he instinctively stiffened to avoid accidental contact. She popped the pod into the top, filled the reservoir from a water bottle, and hit the blinking button. In seconds, the machine sputtered to life, filling the room with the rich, bold scent of roasted coffee.

Cassius watched her blow on her coffee. Something in his chest, which he had not had cause to consult in several centuries, offered an unsolicited opinion. He ignored it. It persisted.

"Here," Rowan said, unaware of his situation. She pulled her travel mug from under the spout and leaned against the counter. "Cyprian should be here soon. But until he arrives, we need a new strategy. If the curse heals overnight, we can't just do one ritual a day. We need constant, sustained presence."

"You are suggesting we hold hands for the entirety of the day?" Cassius asked, the thought sending a phantom spike of agony up his arm.

"I'm suggesting we don't sit on opposite sides of the room pretending the other doesn't exist," she corrected, taking a cautious sip. "Cyprian said the bond thrives on connection. That means we have to actually connect. We need to talk. We need to share space. We need to pretend, even for a few hours, that we are two normal people spending time together, rather than two cursed hostages waiting for the executioner."

Cassius frowned, processing the tactical necessity. "You wish to engage in... domestic activities."

"I wish to have a conversation," she said. She gestured to the sofa. "Sit."

Cassius moved to the sofa, sitting rigidly on the far edge. Rowan walked over and sat on the opposite cushion, pulling her knees up to her chest.

"Tell me something real about yourself," Rowan ordered. "Something that isn't on your official Council dossier. And please, nothing about how many people you've killed. Keep it light."

Cassius stared at his gloved hands, feeling vastly unequipped for this engagement. "I do not have a light history, Rowan. I was forged for a singular purpose. I do not possess hobbies."

"Everyone has something," Rowan pushed gently. "What did you do before the wars?"

"There was always a war," Cassius replied simply. But he saw the annoyance beginning to spark in her eyes, and he hastily searched his incredibly long memory for something that might satisfy her. "There was... a partner. Long ago. Before I was made Commander."

Rowan lowered her coffee. "A romantic partner?"

"A battle partner," Cassius corrected. The distinction was vital to him. "His name was Elias. We fought back-to-back for eighty years. He was the only person who did not flinch when my shadows manifested. He thought they were... amusing."

He paused, a dull ache settling over him. It wasn't the searing pain of the curse; just the quiet, nostalgic ghost of an old friendship. "He fell during an ambush. I was too slow."

He braced himself for the heavy tragedy that usually followed such admissions. Humans enjoyed leaning into the drama.

Instead, Rowan nodded slowly, taking a sip of her coffee. "It sucks when the universe takes the only person who actually gets the joke."

Cassius looked up, surprised by the raw, pragmatic truth in her words. "You speak from experience."

Rowan traced the rim of her coffee mug, offering a small, sad smile. "My fiancÃ©. Three years ago. A car accident." She said it cleanly, without dramatic inflection. "He was an accountant. The most aggressively normal man alive. He thought my job with the Council was just a very intense historical research position. He used to leave extremely bland sandwiches for me when I came home smelling like brimstone."

She let out a short, breathy laugh. "The irony is ridiculous. I spend my life breaking ancient curses, and the thing that takes him out is a patch of black ice."

Cassius looked at her. He mapped the lines of quiet resilience around her eyes. He wanted to cross the small distance between them and pull her against his chest; to shield her from the mundane tragedies of the world. "I am sorry for your loss. I do not know... how to exist comfortably with human grief."

"No one does," Rowan corrected. "You just learn to carry it."

The silence that followed was a different kind from the ones before it.

She set her coffee down. Her expression settled back into professional determination. "Right. That is enough sharing of emotional vulnerabilities for one morning. We need to escalate the ritual. Cyprian said the bond needs maximum proximity."

She looked straight at him. "Holding hands isn't working fast enough. The curse is too deep in my chest. Which means we need to get closer to the heart."

Cassius froze, his pulse skyrocketing. "Rowan. No."

"Cassius," she mocked, mimicking his deep rumble terribly. She stood up and reached for the hem of her thick sweater. "Take your shirt off. We are doing skin-to-skin contact, chest to chest."

"That is completely inappropriate," Cassius choked out, his eyes widening in pure panic. "You cannot simply..."

"I am dying, Cassius!" Rowan yelled, throwing her arms wide in exasperation. She pulled the heavy wool sweater over her head and tossed it onto a chair. Underneath, she wore a simple, fitted black tank top. "I don't care about propriety. I care about outrunning this magical infection. Now take your shirt off and come here."

Cassius felt entirely, hopelessly outmaneuvered. He stood up, his hands shaking slightly as he unbuttoned his dark tactical shirt. He pulled it off, dropping it onto the sofa.

His chest was entirely scarred, marked by centuries of blades and claws, but the most horrifying marks were the chaotic, jagged black veins of the curse, twisting up from his arms and spider-webbing across his pectorals, pointing directly toward his heart.

Rowan swallowed hard when she saw them, her professional facade cracking. "Okay. That looks terrifying. Let's fix it."

"This will be significantly worse than holding hands," Cassius warned gravely. He stepped directly in front of her, his massive frame towering over her smaller one. "The magic will react violently."

"I know," she said, her voice shaking slightly. She placed her uncursed hand flat on the center of his chest.

It was agony instantly. The curse roared to life, perceiving her touch as a direct assault on the host's vital core. White-hot, tearing pain ripped through Cassius, so intense he dropped to his knees, taking Rowan down with him.

But as they hit the concrete floor together, Rowan wrapped her arms around his shoulders, pressing her chest against him.

The pain peaked. Then something broke through it. Not gentle. It hit his sternum like a fist and spread. Not warmth exactly, but presence. The certainty of her, right here, chest to chest, her heartbeat slamming against his. He pulled her closer. It kept spreading.

Cassius buried his face in her neck, a ragged, breathless sound tearing from his throat. He wrapped his massive arms around her waist, holding her against him, feeding the bond with every ounce of his willpower.

When they finally broke apart twenty minutes later, they were both shaking, wrung out, entirely spent. Rowan collapsed back against the side of the sofa, gasping for air.

Cassius pushed himself up, resting on his heels. He checked his chest. The black veins had retreated significantly, at least three inches, pulling back away from his heart and settling into his deltoids. He checked Rowan's hand. The ivy had retreated back past her wrist.

Real progress. But still mathematically inadequate. It was a war of attrition, and they were already deeply exhausted.

Rowan let her head fall back against the upholstery. A strand of hair was stuck to her cheek.

Cassius reached out. He hesitated for a fraction of a second, terrified the pain would return. But he knew, instinctively, that the ritual had fortified the territory. He gently, very carefully, brushed the strand of hair away from her face with his fingertips.

The touch didn't burn. It was just warm skin against warm skin.

Rowan's eyes fluttered open. She looked at him, surprise filtering through her exhaustion.

"It didn't hurt," Cassius whispered in awe.

"Good," Rowan breathed, leaning her cheek slightly into his hand. "Because if you hurt me again, I am writing you up to the Council."

Cassius smiled. He wasn't sure what his face was doing. He let it.

They did not leave the safe house that day. Instead, they fought a grueling, exhaustive war of attrition against the magic festering in their veins. Three more times before the sun finally set, they repeated the skin-to-skin ritual.

Each session stretched longer than the last. Thirty minutes. Forty-five. A full hour. By the fourth, neither of them was counting anymore.

The Shadow Twin bond was doing something to him. He became aware of it gradually, the way you become aware of a tide: not the moment it turns, but when you realize the water is at your knees.

As they sat pressed together on the sofa later that evening, chest to chest for the fourth time, Cassius stared down at the top of her head and very carefully did not think about the things he was thinking about. His shadows, which had spent three centuries being highly professional, were doing something restless and proprietary around the two of them. He noted this. He chose not to examine it further. That seemed like a problem for a man with more time.

That night, Cassius lay in the bed, once again pinned rigidly to the extreme edge of the mattress. Rowan was deeply asleep beside him, her exhaustion pulling her completely under.

Hours passed. The room was silent and freezing.

Cassius shifted, unable to suppress a minor cramp in his side. As he did, his gaze fell on the bare skin of Rowan's outstretched arm.

He froze, the breath vanishing from his lungs.

The black veins on her wrist were no longer receding. They weren't even holding steady through the night. The magic had mutated, reacting aggressively to their evening ritual.

While she slept, the shadowy ink had bypassed her arm entirely in a massive, terrifying leap. A thick, branching network of corruption was currently creeping down from her collarbone, stretching directly over her heart.

The curse wasn't just regenerating. It was accelerating. They barely had two days.

Chapter 4: The Claiming

By the morning of the third day, the curse had stopped being a terrifying, vaguely conceptual magical threat and had downgraded into something far worse: the supernatural equivalent of the world's worst flu.

Rowan woke up feeling terrible. She had no energy, her joints ached, and the black veins had spider-webbed ominously past her collarbone, weaving a jagged pattern just above her heart. She was exhausted in the specific way of someone being eaten alive from the inside, with no amount of sleep able to fix it.

Despite the pain, she didn't want to move. Sometime during the night, Cassius had involuntarily shifted from his rigid, marble-statue sleeping position. His massive arm was now slung heavy over her waist, pulling her flush against his side. Even in sleep, his protective instincts had taken over.

She stared at the wall. The curse marks on her collarbone sat three inches from her heart. Cassius's arm was heavy across her waist.

She carefully extricated herself from his grip, suppressing a wince as her cursed joints flared in protest. By the time Cyprian Valen walked through the reinforced door of the safe house an hour later, Rowan was sitting vertically on the sofa, clutching a mug of aggressively medicated tea.

Cyprian, dressed impeccably in a tailored charcoal suit, evaluated them both with his usual clinical detachment.

"The claiming ritual you performed yesterday slowed the progression, but the magic has mutated," Cyprian announced, dropping a manila folder onto the coffee table. He looked critically at the black veins creeping up Cassius's chest. "The stalling maneuver is failing. If you do not escalate immediately, the curse will reach your hearts by midnight. And then my paperwork triples, which I deeply, personally want to avoid."

Before either of them could formulate a sufficiently sarcastic response regarding their imminent demise, the temperature in the room plummeted by forty degrees.

Frost cracked across the concrete walls in jagged fractals. The hot tea in Rowan's mug iced over and split the ceramic.

"Oh, come on," Rowan groaned, watching her ruined tea spill onto the floor.

A figure stepped out of the frosted shadows in the corner of the room. Glacius Diamante, the Frost Warden of the Council, stood there looking characteristically miserable. He was practically vibrating with cold, his white-blonde hair falling over eyes that looked like frozen lakes.

Cyprian barely glanced at the icy intruder. He buttoned his suit jacket, heading for the door. He paused on the threshold, looking back at Cassius and Rowan with an exasperated sigh.

"Sex magic," Cyprian said flatly. "Today. It is the only way you survive this."

With that horrific bomb dropped, the door clicked shut behind him.

Glacius slowly raised a single, frozen eyebrow at the closed door. The silence in the room was aggressively heavy.

Then, Glacius turned back, his face returning to its usual deadpan expression. He looked from Cassius to Rowan, noting the physical distance between them. "I see you have decided to handle your impending demise with extreme social awkwardness."

Cassius stood up, his massive frame shifting into a defensive posture. "Glacius. Why are you here? Has something happened?"

Glacius sighed, a puff of visible mist escaping his lips. "Always. It is exhausting. Konstantin Shard has mobilized a splinter faction of rebels in the north. Valentina wants you back on the field immediately. She sent me to retrieve you."

"I cannot return," Cassius said, his voice hard. "I am currently bound by a death hex and attempting to salvage this situation."

"Yes. I can see the veins," Glacius said dryly, drifting closer. The cold radiating off him made Rowan pull her sweater tighter around her shoulders. He studied them both for a moment. "And I can feel the bond. It is incredibly loud. It feels like someone is screaming 'mine' directly into my temporal lobe." He paused, looking genuinely annoyed. "Are you two honestly just staring at each other from across the room while actively dying? If this is how modern courtship works, I am glad I live in an ice palace with my sled dogs."

"It's complicated," Rowan managed through chattering teeth. "Also, please stop freezing my furniture. I'm already sick."

She had catalogued him while he stood there. Frost Warden, Council enforcement, the kind of supernatural who made the air hurt. She had questions. This was not the moment for them.

Glacius looked at the frost on the chair and offered a distinctly un-apologetic half-shrug. "My apologies. I have forgotten how fragile humans are. I should return to my dogs. At least they do not require complex emotional rituals to survive."

He turned toward the door. "I will tell Valentina you are indisposed. Try not to die, Cassius. Valentina would not be happy with the need to replace you."

With a blast of freezing wind, Glacius vanished, leaving a small pile of snow on the basement rug.

Rowan stared at the snow. Three days of treating this like a medical quarantine. It hadn't been enough.

But Cyprian was right. They were stalling.

Rowan looked up at Cassius. He was standing near the sofa, clearly fighting the overwhelming urge to apologize for everything that had just happened. He looked exhausted, terrifyingly large, and entirely out of his depth.

"Rowan," Cassius began, his voice dropping into that formal, tragic register he used when he was about to say something noble and infuriating. "I want to reiterate that I will not force you into anything. The claiming ritual is profound. It requires a level of intimacy that should never be coerced by a curse. If you wish to.""

"Cassius," Rowan interrupted, cutting through his brooding monologue. She stood up, tossing the broken pieces of her mug into the trash can. She walked across the room until she was standing directly in front of him.

"Yes?" he asked carefully, leaning down just a fraction.

"Do you actually want this?" Her voice was steady, despite the exhaustion dragging at her bones. "Me? Or are you just trying to survive the week? Because if this is just a very elaborate medical procedure to you, I'm going to pass and take my chances with the magic."

Cassius froze. His eyes flared, the color shifting from their usual pale silver into a deep, consuming black. The shadows in the corners of the room surged forward, responding to the sudden spike in his emotions.

"Medical procedure?" The words tore out of him like a growl. For the first time since she had met him, the careful, polite restraint he always wore cracked entirely.

He moved so fast Rowan didn't even see him step forward. His hands were on her waist, his grip firm and desperate, pulling her flush against his chest. The contact sent a sharp, agonizing stab of the curse through her veins, but it was gone a half-second later, replaced by the bond, immediate and certain.

"Rowan," he breathed, his voice rough and ragged. He leaned down, his forehead resting against hers. "I am terrified. I have spent three centuries being absolutely nothing but a weapon. I do not know how to be a person. I definitely don't know how to be the person you deserve."

He let out a shaky breath. "But if this curse had given us a hundred years instead of seven days, I would have spent every single one of them convincing you over and over again to be mine."

Rowan felt her breath catch. Her heart thumped a wildly irregular rhythm.

She reached up, her hands tangling in his dark hair. "Good to know," she whispered, a breathless smile breaking across her face. "Let's not waste our time, then."

She pulled him down, closing the remaining distance, and kissed him.

The reaction was explosive. The moment their lips met, the bond snapped entirely into place. It wasn't the slow, grinding burn of their earlier rituals. This was faster, fuller, everything the earlier attempts had been straining toward.

Cassius let out a sound that was half-groan, half-growl. He lifted her effortlessly, wrapping her legs around his waist, and carried her the three steps to the bed. He followed her down onto the mattress, his mouth never leaving hers.

He was practically vibrating with a pent-up, ancient need, trying desperately to be gentle while the vampire half of him clearly wanted to devour her. His hands moved with intent, pulling away the heavy wool of her sweater, tracing the lines of her skin as if committing them to memory.

"Cassius," Rowan gasped as he broke the kiss to trail his lips down her jaw, his fangs grazing the sensitive skin of her neck just enough to send a wild thrill of adrenaline through her. "You are functionally immortal. Stop acting like we only have three minutes."

He pulled back, his eyes dark and dilated, a flush of color high on his cheekbones. For a moment, he just stared at her, his chest heaving. Then something shifted in his expression. The frantic desperation smoothed into something more deliberate, more focused.

"You're right," he murmured, his voice dropping an octave. "We have time." His thumb traced her lower lip with aching slowness. "And I intend to use every second of it."

He kissed her again, but this time it was different. Slower. Deeper. His mouth moved against hers with the kind of attention that suggested he was learning her, cataloging every response. When she made a soft sound in the back of her throat, he repeated the exact motion that had caused it, filing the information away like the strategic genius he was.

His hands slid under her sweater with deliberate care, palms warm against her ribs. "May I?" he asked against her mouth, his fingers already curled in the fabric.

"Yes," she breathed. "God, yes."

He pulled the sweater over her head in one smooth motion, tossing it somewhere behind him. His eyes darkened as he took her in, the simple black bra, the curse marks still faintly visible on her collarbone, the rapid rise and fall of her chest.

"Rowan," he said, her name coming out like a prayer. His fingertips traced the edge of the curse mark, and where he touched, warmth bloomed. "You are extraordinary."

"You're wearing too many clothes for this level of compliment," she managed, tugging at his tactical shirt.

A ghost of a smile crossed his face, that rare, rusty expression that made her heart do inconvenient things. He sat back on his heels and pulled the shirt over his head in one fluid motion.

Rowan's breath caught.

She'd felt his body pressed against hers, knew he was built like someone who'd spent centuries in combat, but seeing him was different. The curse marks were still visible, dark veins spreading from his heart, but they were already fading at the edges where her touch had reached him.

"Oh," she said intelligently.

His mouth quirked. "Is that approval or concern?"

"Approval," she confirmed, reaching up to trace one of the scars across his ribs. "Definite approval. Also mild concern that you're going to break the bed frame."

"I will buy a new one," he said seriously, catching her hand and pressing a kiss to her palm. The gesture was so unexpectedly tender that it made her chest ache.

Then his hands moved to the button of her jeans. "May I?" he asked again, his fingers pausing.

"If you ask permission one more time, I'm going to file a formal complaint with the Council about your commitment to bureaucracy," Rowan said, lifting her hips to help him.

He actually laughed, a real one, low and rough and surprised. "Duly noted."

He slid her jeans down her legs with careful efficiency, his hands skimming her thighs in a way that made her shiver. When they joined her sweater on the floor, he paused, his gaze traveling over her with an intensity that should have been uncomfortable but instead felt like being seen for the first time in years.

"You're staring," she pointed out, fighting the urge to cover herself.

"I am memorizing," he corrected, his fingers trailing up her calf, over her knee, along her inner thigh with devastating slowness. "I have spent three hundred years alone, Rowan. Allow me this."

The vulnerability in his voice undid her. "Okay," she whispered. "But I get to memorize too."

"Deal."

She reached for his belt, and he went very still, watching her with an expression that was equal parts anticipation and barely leashed control. She worked the buckle free, then the button of his pants, hyperaware of the way his breathing had gone shallow. When she slid the zipper down, he made a sound low in his throat that sent heat pooling in her stomach.

He stood just long enough to kick off his boots and strip off the rest of his clothes, and then he was back, covering her body with his, skin to skin. The contact sent a jolt through the bond, a golden rush of sensation that made them both gasp.

"I can feel you," Rowan breathed, her hands sliding up his back. "Not just physically. I can feel..."

"Everything," Cassius finished, his forehead dropping to hers. "I know. I feel you too." His voice roughened. "Your warmth. Your life. Your..." He broke off, something like wonder crossing his face. "Your joy."

"You sound surprised."

"I am. I had forgotten what it felt like." He kissed her softly, almost reverently. "Thank you for reminding me."

Then his mouth began to travel. He kissed his way down her jaw, her neck, pausing to scrape his fangs gently over her pulse point in a way that made her arch against him. When he reached the curve of her breast, he looked up at her, a question in his eyes.

"Yes," she said, threading her fingers through his hair. "Yes, Cassius."

He unhooked her bra with surprising dexterity for someone who'd been touch-starved for centuries, and then his mouth was on her, hot and demanding. Every touch sent feedback through the bond, she could feel his pleasure at her response, his deep satisfaction at making her gasp and squirm. It was overwhelming and perfect and not nearly enough.

"Lower," she managed, tugging at his hair. "Cassius, I need..."

"Tell me," he said against her skin, his hands spanning her waist. "Tell me what you need."

"Lower," she repeated, her face flushing. "I need you lower."

Understanding dawned in his eyes, along with something that looked a lot like hunger. "As you wish."

He kissed his way down her stomach, pausing to trace each of her rune tattoos with his tongue like he was reading them. When he reached the waistband of her underwear, he hooked his fingers in the fabric and looked up at her one more time.

"Please," she said, and that was all the permission he needed.

He pulled them off and settled between her thighs, his hands gripping her hips with careful strength. For a moment, he just looked at her, and Rowan fought the urge to close her legs against the intensity of his gaze.

"You are perfect," he said quietly. Then he leaned down and put his mouth on her.

The first touch of his tongue made her cry out, her hips jerking against his hold. He made a satisfied sound and did it again, slower this time, learning her the way he'd learned her mouth, with total focus and devastating attention to detail.

It was good. Really good. But he was being too careful, too gentle, like he was afraid she'd break.

"Cassius," she gasped, her fingers tightening in his hair. "You can, more pressure. Right there. Yes, like that."

He followed her instructions with the dedication of a man on a mission, adjusting his technique based on every sound she made, every shift of her hips. When he added his fingers, curling them inside her while his mouth worked, the sensation amplified through the bond until she couldn't tell where her pleasure ended and his satisfaction began.

"Oh god," she panted, her thighs trembling. "Don't stop, don't"

He didn't. He kept the exact pressure, the exact rhythm, until the tension coiling in her stomach finally snapped. She came with a broken cry, her back arching off the bed as waves of pleasure crashed through her, doubled by the bond, by feeling his fierce joy at her release.

When she finally came back to herself, he was pressing soft kisses to her inner thigh, his expression dazed and deeply smug.

"That was," she started, then gave up on words. "Come here."

He crawled back up her body, and she could taste herself on his mouth when she kissed him. His cock was hard against her hip, and she reached down to wrap her hand around him, earning a strangled groan.

"Rowan," he gritted out, his hips jerking into her touch. "I need."

"I know," she said, guiding him to her entrance. "I need it too."

He pushed inside slowly, his eyes locked on hers, and the sensation was almost too much. Not just the physical stretch and fullness, but the emotional weight of it, the bond singing between them, the way she could feel his overwhelming relief and wonder and desperate need to be gentle even though every instinct was screaming at him to move.

"Breathe," she whispered, cupping his face. "I'm not going to break."

"You are the most precious thing I have ever held," he said roughly, his voice cracking. "Forgive me if I am cautious."

"You're perfect," she assured him, wrapping her legs around his waist. "Now move. Please."

He did, pulling back and sliding home again with a controlled thrust that made them both moan. Each movement felt right. Like something that had always been true, finally allowed to be.

"My Rowan," he breathed against her neck, his rhythm steady and deep.

The words undid her. She clung to him, meeting each thrust, feeling the building pleasure through both their perspectives the way her body gripped him, the way he filled her completely, the overwhelming rightness of it.

The dual sensation, internal and external, physical and emotional, pushed her right to the precipice. As she hovered there, Cassius let out a guttural sound and sank his fangs into the sensitive curve of her neck. The sudden, sharp bite and the intoxicating pull as he took a mouthful of her blood short-circuited her brain entirely, throwing her over the edge into a complete, world-ending release. She cried out his name, arching off the bed, and the sheer force of her release pulled him with her. He buried himself deep with a hoarse shout, his body shuddering violently as he spilled inside her.

Cassius collapsed against her, his weight pressing her into the mattress. He slowly withdrew his fangs, his mouth lingering to drag his tongue over the puncture wounds and seal them. His massive arms wrapped around her like he was afraid she'd disappear, and she could feel him trembling, whether from exertion, emotion, or the overwhelming rush of her blood, she wasn't sure. Probably all three.

"Are you okay?" she asked, running her fingers through his sweat-damp hair.

"I am." He stopped, his voice rough. "I do not have words, Rowan. I feel everything. Your warmth. Your presence in my mind. The absence of pain for the first time in weeks." He lifted his head to look at her, and his eyes were suspiciously bright. "Everything is different."

She smiled, her own eyes stinging. "Good. Because you're stuck with me now."

"There is nowhere I would rather be," he said seriously, then paused. "Although perhaps we should move at some point. I am likely crushing you."

"You're fine," she assured him, tightening her hold. "Stay."

So he did, their bodies still joined, the bond humming contentedly between them as the curse marks retreated, pulling all the way back up to her shoulder joint.

An hour later, the basement was quiet.

"It didn't break it completely," Rowan said, tracing the faded edges of the remaining dark marks on her arm. A sharp twinge of reality. They had dealt a massive blow to the curse, stalling its march to their hearts, but the infection was stubborn.

"It bought us time," Cassius rumbled, pressing a kiss to the top of her messy hair. "We pushed it back significantly. We have hope now, Rowan. It is no longer a death sentence."

"We'll have to deal with the root of it tomorrow," she agreed, leaning into his warmth. "But... I feel incredible right now. Physically. Magically." She propped herself up on an elbow. "Through the bond, I felt, well. Everything."

Cassius blinked, a sudden look of horror crossing his features. "Everything?"

"Everything," Rowan confirmed, a slow, wicked grin spreading across her face. "I felt your loneliness. I felt your hope. And most importantly, I caught a glimpse of your apartment from your memories. Cassius, did you seriously decorate your living room in 'Early Century Dungeon' chic? Are those actual velvet curtains?"

Cassius let out a long, heavy sigh, letting his head thump back against the pillows. The fearsome Nyx Breaker, completely defeated by his own interior design choices. "They are practical. They block the sun."

"They look like they belong in a haunted Victorian rectory," Rowan corrected, lying back down and snuggling comfortably against his side. "When we finally cure this thing completely, I am taking you to IKEA. Your next combat mission is going to involve assembling a Hemnes dresser."

"I look forward to the battle," he murmured, his arms tightening around her. And for the first time in centuries, he actually meant it.

Chapter 5: The Witch's Revenge

For the first time in three hundred and twelve years, Cassius woke up to find that his bed was not a cold, solitary slab of tactical resting.

It was warm. It smelled of cheap safehouse soap and warm skin. The massive, crushing weight of the centuries that usually sat on his chest the moment he opened his eyes was suspiciously absent. Instead, there was just the bond, steady and warm, tuned to the rhythm of the heartbeat of the woman tangled in his arms.

Rowan was asleep, her face pressed against his collarbone, her legs thoroughly entwined with his. The dark, jagged veins of the death hex had retreated entirely from her neck and chest, hovering around her shoulder joint.

Cassius lay perfectly still, staring at the concrete ceiling of the basement. He was experiencing a sensation so foreign he almost couldn't identify it.

He was content.

He, the lethally efficient, emotionally stunted Nyx Breaker, was actually, stupidly happy in a safehouse basement while a witch's curse pulsed in his veins.

The realization was staggering. He tightened his hold on Rowan just slightly, marveling, somewhat against his will, at how correctly she fit against him. He briefly considered never leaving this bed again. Perhaps they could simply order takeout for the next hundred years.

Then, the universe decided he had experienced enough joy for one century.

Rowan violently thrashed against him. The bond lurched sideways into something cold and wrong.

"Rowan!" Cassius barked, his combat instincts snapping him fully awake. He sat up, his vampire speed allowing him to narrowly avoid a frantic elbow aimed directly at his jaw.

She was gasping, her spine locked in an unnatural arch, eyes tracking rapid behind their lids. But worse than the thrashing was the curse mark on her shoulder. The dormant black veins were no longer fading; they were bleeding a thick, suffocating black mist into the air, swirling with the foul stench of ozone and ancient rot.

The Witch.

Cassius didn't hesitate. He grabbed Rowan by the shoulders, grounding her with his massive strength, and forcefully pushed his forehead against hers. He threw his magical presence across the bond, slamming open the metaphysical door into her mind.

He immediately caught the backwash of the vision.

He found himself standing in a desolate, ash-covered void. The air tasted permanently of decay. Standing in the center of the wasteland was a withered, terrifying spectral figure wearing seventeenth-century rags, clutching a gnarled staff. The Witch of Salem, her mouth wide open in a furious, ear-splitting shriek about inescapable doom, eternal rot, and the folly of defying her hex.

Cassius was not horrified. He wasn't triggered into a panic by the sheer display of ghostly dominance.

Instead, a raw, quiet fury settled in him as he watched the curse torture the woman in his arms.

You are trespassing, Cassius thought, his voice echoing through the void with absolute, cold authority. *And you are threatening the only thing in this universe I intend to keep.*

He drove the bond through the void like a battering ram, slamming it directly into the Witch's spectral projection. She didn't shatter immediately. For three long seconds, she held. Then the force obliterated the ash-covered void, violently ejecting her from Rowan's mind.

Rowan's eyes snapped open. She gasped for air, her fingers digging painfully into Cassius's forearms as she collapsed against his chest, shaking uncontrollably.

"I've got you," Cassius murmured, his voice infinitely gentler than the one he had just used to verbally assault a ghost in the astral plane. He ran a large hand up and down her spine, pressing a kiss to her temple. "She is gone. You are safe."

"She's so... loud," Rowan whispered, swallowing hard. She pressed her face into his neck, letting out a shaky breath. "And she is really, really angry that we slowed the progression of the curse with our... extracurricular activities."

Cassius's jaw tightened. "She is throwing a temper tantrum because she is losing. She is an annoyance, Rowan. Nothing more."

"An annoyance that lives in our bloodstreams," Rowan pointed out, finally pulling back just enough to look at him. She looked pale and exhausted again, the brief respite of the night stolen from her. "I think she's going to accelerate her tactics immediately."

An hour later, Cyprian Valen stepped cautiously into the basement. He was carrying his usual tablet, a stark white cardboard box from a high-end bakery, and an expression of distinct disapproval.

Cassius and Rowan were sitting at the small kitchenette table. Rowan was nursing her third cup of the safehouse's terrible coffee, while Cassius was methodically peeling an apple with a disturbingly sharp tactical knife.

"The physical escalation of the curse has been successfully halted by your claiming ritual," Cyprian announced, setting the bakery box on the table. "Congratulations on surviving the night. I brought croissants to celebrate not having to file death certificates."

"Thank you, Cyprian," Rowan said dryly, taking a croissant. "However, the Witch decided to show up in my head this morning to scream at me about eternal rot."

Cyprian sighed, pulling out a slim stylus and tapping a few aggressive notes into his tablet. "I suspected as much. The biological threat is neutralized, but the curse has unfortunately entrenched itself. It is semi-sentient. It recognized it was losing the physical war against your bond, so it retreated into the metaphysical anchor of the hex."

"English, Cyprian," Rowan requested, rubbing her temples.

"It means," Cyprian said, "that the curse will no longer try to stop your hearts. Instead, it will simply lie dormant, creating a secondary magical infection that will slowly eat your sanity from the inside out through constant psychic attacks." Cyprian looked up, adjusting his glasses. "Which means you have to go into a trance to fight her ghost directly."

Cassius stopped peeling the apple. He looked slowly from the tactical knife to Cyprian. "You want us to voluntarily enter an astral void to battle a seventeenth-century witch on her own metaphysical territory?"

"Yes," Cyprian confirmed. "If you do not root her out from the inside, you will both be institutionalized within a month. I will return tomorrow evening with the required hallucinatory potion to induce the shared trance." He tucked his tablet under his arm. "Try to spend the day establishing protective wards. The stronger your anchor in the physical world, the less likely she is to trap your souls in the void forever."

Before either of them could respond to that horrifying caveat, Cyprian was already opening the heavy steel door. "Have a productive day," he said, and vanished into the stairwell.

Neither of them moved for a moment.

"I am going to throw his tablet into a river," Cassius said.

"I'll help you," Rowan agreed.

The rest of the day was spent preparing the basement for a supernatural war. It shouldn't have been fun. They were actively preparing to face an evil entity that had been haunting their veins for four days. And yet, the afternoon quickly devolved into a surprisingly domestic sort of chaos.

They were forced to actually work together as a cohesive unit, a dynamic they fell into with startling ease. Rowan spent an hour using thick white chalk to draw massive salt runes on the basement floor, following a diagram Cyprian had left behind.

Cassius, however, could not handle her artistic execution.

"That is not a perfect circle, Rowan," Cassius pointed out, crossing his arms over his chest. His tactical, centuries-old brain was deeply, fundamentally offended by her asymmetrical sweeping motions. "The ward will leak. That geometry is structurally unsound."

Rowan paused, chalk dust all over her black jeans, and blew a strand of hair out of her face. "It's a metaphysical magical barrier, Cassius, not an architectural blueprint for a bridge. The intention is what matters."

"The geometry matters," Cassius insisted, stepping forward.

Rowan held the chalk out to him in a blatant challenge. "You want to try it, Geometry Boy?"

Cassius snatched the chalk. In three seconds flat, using a blur of vampire speed that made Rowan blink, he swept across the floor, drawing a flawlessly, mathematically precise circle that would have made a drafting compass jealous.

He stood up, dusting his hands off with a highly satisfied look. "Proper perimeter secured."

Rowan rolled her eyes, but she couldn't hide the intensely fond smile breaking across her face. "You are such an unbelievable nerd. An immortal, lethal, terrifying nerd."

"I am precise," he corrected, though the corner of his mouth twitched upward.

Later that afternoon, Cyprian returned briefly to drop off more specialized herbs for the ritual. Rowan headed to the tiny bathroom to wash the chalk and salt dust off her hands, leaving Cassius and Cyprian alone in the basement.

Cyprian stood near the mathematically perfect chalk circle, tapping his very expensive pen against his clipboard.

"She is remarkably resilient," Cyprian noted casually, watching Cassius methodically place protective black candles around the perimeter.

"She is extraordinary," Cassius replied immediately, his tone brokering absolutely no argument.

"She is also very, very mortal," Cyprian said dryly.

Cassius stopped moving. He looked at Cyprian, the easy domesticity of the afternoon vanishing in an instant.

"If you survive this trance tomorrow," Cyprian continued, his voice devoid of its usual snark, "the curse breaks. Completely. Which means Rowan goes back to her normal, highly breakable human life. She ages. She gets sick. And you continue being a three-hundred-year-old immortal weapon who does not age a day." Cyprian met Cassius's eyes with a look of genuine, exhausted sympathy. "That is a logistical nightmare waiting to happen, Cassius."

Cassius remained perfectly still, the unlit candle gripped tightly in his massive hand.

The weight of Cyprian's words settled over him. He hadn't thought past surviving the week. But now, looking at the closed bathroom door, the thought of letting her age, fade, or walk away back into a world where he couldn't protect her was physically sickening.

It felt like a second curse.

He didn't say anything to Cyprian, but when the door clicked shut behind the administrator, Cassius was left standing in the center of the basement, his heart pounding a frantic, desperate rhythm.

He set the candle down. He didn't light it.

That evening, the wards were drawn. The protections were set. Tomorrow night, they would drink Cyprian's potion and enter the void. This was their last night of relative normalcy.

They were sitting side-by-side on the terrible plaid sofa. Rowan looked exhausted, her head resting on Cassius's shoulder. Cassius had an arm wrapped securely around her waist, pulling her flush against his side, silently anchoring her to the physical world.

"Are you terrified?" Rowan asked, her fingers lightly tracing the faded black lines of the curse mark on his forearm.

Cassius rested his chin on the top of her head. "Of a dead witch who relies on cheap theatricality to terrify her victims? No," he said honestly. "But I am terrified of what happens after."

Rowan shifted, looking up at him with a slight frown. "Cassius..."

He shifted on the sofa so he could look at her fully.

"I do not regret a single second of this absolute catastrophe," he said, his voice dropping into that low, serious rumble that made a shiver chase down Rowan's spine. "Not the agonizing pain, not the impending doom, not the horrifying psychic attacks at seven in the morning, and certainly not the terrible safehouse coffee."

He reached up, his large, battle-scarred hand cupping her face with devastating gentleness. His thumb brushed over her cheekbone.

"I have spent three centuries in rooms like this one, Rowan," he whispered, all of his walls crashing down at once. "You are the only thing in three centuries that has made the rest of it feel worth the inconvenience." He leaned in closer, his gaze dropping to her lips. "Whatever happens inside that trance tomorrow... whatever she tries to do or say to break us apart... know that you are mine. And I am entirely, irrevocably yours."

Rowan's breath caught in her throat. Her eyes stung with sudden, hot tears.

She smiled and kissed him, a slow, tender, anchoring kiss that pushed back the lingering chill of the witch's magic and sealed the promise between them.

Cassius pulled her onto his lap, wrapping both arms around her, refusing to let even an inch of space exist between them. They slept gathered around the quiet steadiness of the bond between them.

Chapter 6: Into the Curse

The potion smelled like cremated holiday candles.

I mentioned this to Cyprian, who looked at me with the expression of a man who had long since given up adjusting his expectations for his clients.

"It is not meant to be pleasant," he said. He was holding two small stone vials, one for each of us, with the careful precision of someone handling something that could level a city block. "It triggers a shared trance state that will align your consciousness with the metaphysical frequency of the curse. The experience will feel entirely real. The physical dangers are also entirely real."

"Great," I said.

"If you let go of each other's hands at any point, your souls will become unmoored from your physical anchor." He glanced between us with tremendous professional detachment. "That is a permanent situation."

I checked the blade at my belt while he talked, a quiet, habitual motion, the way you rattle your keys before a long drive. Still there. Still ready.

"So hold hands," Cassius said. "Understood."

"Also," Cyprian added, picking up his bag with a distinct air of someone who intended to be standing well to the side of whatever happened next, "do not let her talk you into anything. The Witch's ghost is semi-sentient. She has been inhabiting this curse for six months. She knows your psychological profiles better than you do."

He set the vials on the edge of the salt circle, made a short, efficient note on his tablet, and retreated to the far corner of the basement. I got the impression Cyprian attended a lot of potentially fatal supernatural rituals and had simply learned to bring work.

Cassius and I looked at each other across the salt circle. He had already positioned himself in the center, lying flat, arms relaxed at his sides, every inch of him projecting a soldier's calm readiness. If he was terrified, the only sign was the slight tension in his jaw.

"On three?" I said.

"On three," he agreed.

I took my vial. It was warm, which seemed unnecessary. Everything about curses, I had decided, was calibrated to be as unpleasant as possible.

I lay down beside him on the concrete floor. His hand found mine immediately, no hesitation, just the warm, certain press of his palm against my palm. I interlaced our fingers.

We drank.

The basement dissolved like wet watercolor paper.

The void arrived all at once.

The curse realm materialized around us as a colonial New England wasteland frozen in permanent winter. Bare black trees clawed at a sky the color of a bruise. Ash drifted in lazy, impossible spirals. The ground underfoot was glass-hard frozen dirt, and the whole landscape throbbed, when I blinked open my aura sight, that rhythm became visible, a deep crimson beat running through every surface. The Witch's signature. Thick and ancient and furious.

Structurally, actually, it was impressive. An entire semi-sentient curse realm constructed from dying hatred and spite. Some part of me wanted to take notes.

The rest of me was very aware that Cassius was still beside me, solid and real, his hand locked around mine. The bond between us hummed quietly even here, a thread of warmth running against all that crimson. I focused on it.

Small comfort, I thought. *Stupid comfort. I'll take it.*

"Aura readings?" Cassius asked, his voice low.

"She's everywhere," I said. "Every surface. The trees, the ground. She's threaded herself through the whole structure." I turned, scanning the perimeter. "There at the center of the clearing. She's densest there."

He looked where I pointed. His hand tightened around mine.

The Witch arrived with maximum theatrical timing.

She came screaming.

Not in fear. In fury, a rising, ear-splitting shriek that cracked through the frozen air like breaking ice, and she coalesced from the ash itself: a spectral figure in seventeenth-century rags, her face a mask of centuries of grievances, one skeletal hand clutching a gnarled staff. She was objectively terrifying. She was also, somehow, deeply exhausting to look at.

The monologue began immediately.

Doomed love. Arrogant fools. The folly of defying a dying hex. The inevitable rot of all connections. The universe's fundamental indifference to human suffering. She had clearly been rehearsing.

I catalogued her threat level while she talked. Significant magical residue, crimson, complex, layered. The structural architecture of the curse was blood-binding work, which I recognized immediately because Helena had made me memorize the entire taxonomy of sacrifice-tethered hexes before she let me touch my first live case. Blood curses were closed systems. They ran on the original caster's will, anchored in her blood. The only thing that could supersede a blood binding was a more powerful blood bond made voluntarily, the kind that the universe itself recognized as real.

The Shadow Twin bond was exactly that. It just needed proof.

I had been carrying the blade for three days.

She stopped mid-sentence.

I realized I had been frowning at her with professional assessment instead of cowering, and she had noticed.

The temperature dropped another ten degrees.

Her head tilted, slow and predatory, and then her gaze, what passed for eyes in a spectral entity fueled entirely by spite, moved from Cassius to me. It stayed.

"You," she said. The voice had changed. Quieter. More deliberate. A voice that had learned to use stillness as a weapon. "You are the interesting one."

Beside me, Cassius went absolutely still. Not the stillness of fear, I knew what that looked like on him. This was something else. This was a man who had decided her choice mattered more than his survival, and was staying out of the way to prove it.

I filed that information away.

"I've been called worse," I said pleasantly.

The Witch drifted closer. The ash swirled around her like a skirt. "You did not have to take his curse. You chose it. You could choose differently now." A pause. "Let him go. Let the curse complete its work on him. I will lift it from your veins tonight – clean, total, free. You walk out of here unmarked." Her voice dropped further. "You have already lost enough to magic you could not control. You do not have to lose yourself too."

The silence afterward was enormous.

The Witch had done her homework. Six months inside the curse, six months inside Cassius's blood, and somehow she had found the exact shape of what I was afraid of and built a doorway out of it.

My chest did the thing it had been doing since my fiancé died, that specific, hollow seize, the one that lived behind my sternum and only woke up when something hit a direct nerve. I was aware of it, the way you're aware of an old fracture in bad weather. I let it be there. I didn't fight it.

To my left: Cassius. Still. Quiet. Not looking at me, because he would not look at me during this. He would not make this harder than it already was by letting me see his face.

The bond pulsed once. Warm and steady. Not a pull. Not a plea. Just – *present.*

I thought about my fiancé. I thought about Helena. I thought about every person I had loved and lost to magic I couldn't control, and I thought about the very precise, very clinical way I had spent the years afterward making sure I didn't have to feel that again.

Then I thought about the last five days in a damp safe house basement with a five-hundred-year-old vampire who didn't understand espresso machines and drew geometrically perfect salt circles out of sheer compulsive personality.

I looked at the Witch.

"He's an idiot," I said.

Her expression shifted, a flicker of something that looked like triumph. She started to smile.

"But he's my idiot," I continued, "and I have tried, extensively, the strategy of letting people go to keep myself safe. I have a very solid data set on how that works out." I reached for the small ritual blade at my belt with my free hand, the one I had absolutely brought because I am a professional and professionals prepare for contingencies. "It's a bad strategy. I'm retiring it."

The Witch went absolutely silent.

Then she came apart.

Not metaphorically. The spectral shape of her *unraveled* - grief and fury shredding through the bonds of her composure all at once, and she hit the realm like a detonation. The trees didn't just crack; they *exploded*, bark and black splinters screaming outward in every direction. The ash cyclone went vertical, a column of it slamming upward into the bruised sky, tearing the cloud cover open in a ragged wound that bled something darker than dark underneath. The temperature dropped so fast it stole the breath from my lungs.

She came at us.

Not drifting. *Charging* - a spectral freight train of six months of rage, her form burning so hot with crimson curse-light that the air around her scorched. I had a half-second to register that she was done with clever tactics and had moved directly into violence when Cassius stepped in front of me.

He hit her force with his shadow magic, a wall of it slamming up between us and the Witch – not elegant, not refined, the curse-corrupted version of his power that hurt him to use. It held. She screamed against it, clawing at the barrier, the crimson of her light eating at the edges.

"*Now*," Cassius said through his teeth.

Right. The plan. Blood curse, blood bond, Shadow Twin. Three variables. One solution. I'd done riskier things in smaller windows.

The blade was already in my hand. I grabbed his free right hand, the one not burning with the effort of holding the ward, turned it palm-up and drew the blade across it in one clean stroke. He didn't flinch. He took the blade from me immediately and did the same to me, a quick, precise cut across my left palm, the one already interlaced with his. It stung. I ignored it.

The shadow ward cracked. The Witch *howled.*

I slammed my cut palm against his cut palm, both held simultaneously, the old grip and the new one, blood meeting blood at the center where the curse had always lived.

Not because I was brave. Because I had read Helena's notes on blood-binding architecture seventeen times in the last four days and I knew exactly what this would do.

"My life is yours," I said. My voice came out steady, which I considered a personal achievement given the circumstance. "Whatever that means. Whatever it costs." I met his eyes, silver-violet, ancient, currently very focused on me. "Don't make me regret it."

"You never will," he said.

I believed him. That was the part that absolutely terrified me, and also the part that made everything else make sense.

The golden light detonated.

I felt it before I heard it.

It came from our joined hands first, a sudden, bone-deep warmth that tore outward in a shockwave and hit everything. The sound it made was enormous: cathedral bells struck all at once. The crimson pulsing of the curse realm slammed against it and *shattered.* The Witch's scream was the loudest thing I had ever heard, and then it was the quietest, and then it was nothing.

The realm collapsed.

I woke up staring at the cracked concrete ceiling of the basement.

Everything was silent.

Not the silence of the void, the ordinary, slightly damp silence of a poorly ventilated underground room.

I lifted my left arm and looked at it.

Clean. Unmarked. The rune tattoos were exactly where they were supposed to be, sharp and dark and mine. Where the black veins had been spreading for five days: nothing. Just skin.

Beside me, Cassius made a sound.

It was brief and low and entirely undignified, something between an exhaled breath and a very surprised noise, and it was the most un-stoic thing I had heard him produce in five days of shared agony. He was staring at his own hands the way I had stared at mine.

"Gone," he said.

"Gone," I confirmed.

He turned his head and looked at me. I looked back. There was a long moment of mutual, profoundly exhausted silence. The gist of it: *that happened, we survived it, I would like to lie here for approximately one hundred years.*

Cyprian appeared at the edge of the circle. He looked at our clasped, blood-smeared hands. He looked at our unmarked skin. He opened his tablet with the sound of a man who takes no pleasure in being right but is, professionally, required to document it regardless.

"Curse: resolved," he said.

"That's it?" I asked.

"For the curse, yes." He made a note. His pen clicked. "Congratulations. You have done something I have not seen achieved in six hundred years of practice, and I hope neither of you ever need to speak to me again in a professional capacity." He tucked the tablet under his arm and reached for his coat. Then, with his back to us and his voice extremely carefully neutral, he added: "The curse is broken. Which means she is fully human again. Entirely human." A pause. "The logistical problem is still on the table."

He left.

The steel door clicked shut behind him.

Cassius and I lay in the empty salt circle and looked at each other in the ringing silence, our hands still tangled together.

Neither of us moved.

But his thumb moved across my knuckles, slow, careful, deliberate, and I thought: *whatever it is, we'll figure it out.*

Chapter 7: The Choice & The Fall

The curse was gone.

I kept checking. The way you probe a wound to confirm it's healed, a soldier's habit, an old one. My hand to my sternum. No burn. No pull. No countdown ticking behind my ribs like a second heartbeat.

Nothing.

I had spent six months learning to live with a death sentence in my chest, and I did not know what to do with the silence it left behind.

Cyprian conducted his scan with the efficiency of a man billing by the quarter-hour. He confirmed, in clinical terms, that the curse had been fully and permanently broken in both hosts. Rowan's vital signs: healthy, human, stable. He closed his tablet. He looked at me across the salt circle with an expression that occupied the same general neighborhood as both sympathy and respect, without being either.

"Well done," he said. Which, from Cyprian, was essentially a standing ovation.

Then he left.

The basement was quiet.

The salt circle was scuffed from when we'd scrambled upright, the chalk runes smeared at the edges. The whole space smelled of beeswax and old ash and cheap soap.

Everything was exactly as it had been six hours ago. Except we were both alive. And the clock had stopped.

Rowan was sitting on the edge of the bed, silver-blonde hair loose from whatever it had been pinned in, rune tattoos dark against her pale forearms. She was examining the cut on her left palm with the focused attention of someone cataloguing data points. Already closing. She logged it and moved on.

I stood near the door and tried to determine how to say the thing I had been preparing to say for two days.

Soldiers rehearse. I had a thorough speech ready for the moment the curse broke and she had a choice in front of her.

I began it.

"You don't have to stay."

She looked up.

I pressed forward before I lost the structure. "The bond is intact, it's permanent, it won't dissolve, but it doesn't compel you. Nothing in the Shadow Twin bond forces proximity. I looked into it." I had spent most of Day 4 looking into it, between ritual preparation and trying to appear as though I was not. "You could return to your loft. Your work. The bond would recede over time. Become manageable. Something you carry, not something that governs you."

I stopped. The speech had run longer than intended. I was looking at the floor.

"Over time," I added.

The silence stretched long enough that I catalogued the floor in considerable detail.

"Are you done?" Rowan said.

I was.

"Good." She set her hand flat on her knee. "I'm not doing this twice. I choose you. Forever." Stated. Decided. Filed. "And I would like to do that before I talk myself out of it, so if you could please stop being noble for five minutes and tell me how this works."

"Rowan."

"Because I've read the theory but the practical application..."

"Rowan."

She stopped.

I had crossed the room. I didn't remember deciding to. My hand was cupping her face, and she was looking up at me, serious the way she was only when she was telling the truth, the frantic mechanical quality of her thinking gone still, everything else set aside.

"Are you certain," I said. An assessment, not a question.

She gave me the look she reserved for statements she considered beneath her intelligence. Then she reached up and covered my hand with hers.

"Obviously," she said. "Or I wouldn't have said it."

Something in my chest let go. Five centuries of moving from war to war alone, six months of dying by inches, five days of this woman. Released, all at once. Just: done.

I exhaled.

"All right," I said. "I'll explain what happens."

She asked two very good questions and one alarming one. I answered all three. She listened with the focused attention of someone committed to retaining every word, which was the most Rowan thing she could have done, and I found it so specifically, completely her that I had to look away.

The conversion itself was quick for me to perform. I had done it twice before as a sanctioned action by the Council, both deliberate, solemn, nothing like this, which involved Rowan making a dry remark about the professional irony of a curse-breaker becoming a vampire. I almost smiled. She noticed.

And then she was settled in the bed, and still, and the heartbeat I had been listening to for five days was gone.

The bond didn't break. It just went quiet.

That was the part they didn't tell you when they described conversion in clinical terms. The draining was quick; the waiting was not. She was technically dead. Her chest did not rise. The bond, which had been humming warm and constant since the moment it formed, went quiet, not severed, just... suspended, like a held breath. Present. Not gone. But not alive in any way I had a framework for.

I knew, with certainty, that the silence was the process and not the failure.

I also knew that I had never done it like this. She lay still in a basement bed and gave me nothing to act on and no enemy to fight and no problem I could solve by being better at my job.

I lasted four minutes before I stood up.

I rearranged the blanket. It had been correctly arranged. I rearranged it again. I checked the door. I checked the wards on the walls, still intact, no longer necessary, but I checked them anyway. I retrieved a glass of water from the kitchenette and placed it on the floor beside the bed. A logical precaution for a woman who would shortly have heightened physical needs.

I stood at the foot of the bed and counted ceiling tiles.

I retrieved a second pillow from the far corner and placed it near her head. Assessed the arrangement. Suboptimal placement. I adjusted it. Stood back. Reconsidered. Adjusted it again.

I had stood at Lepanto. I had survived the Salem incident of 1692 with my faculties intact, which was, in retrospect, applicable experience given the events of the past week. I had dismantled a god-tier curse network in Prague without losing a man.

Forty-five minutes of biological process was going to be what destroyed me.

I went and got a third pillow.

I needed air.

Technically irrational. I did not require ventilation in the way mortals did. But the basement was four hundred square feet, Rowan was unconscious in it, and I was approximately thirty seconds from reorganizing the kitchenette out of sheer necessity. I went up the stairs and through the heavy exterior door.

The night was cold. Minneapolis had determined that tonight was not yet the night spring arrived. The air was cold and smelled of city winter. I stood on the concrete steps and ran a threat assessment from reflex.

"You're alive."

Glacius Diamante was positioned against the building wall with the stillness of a man who had been there for some time and found the wait entirely acceptable. Frost sat in his platinum hair and on the shoulders of his coat. He had not knocked.

"Apparently," I said.

He studied me. Then something shifted in his expression, barely perceptible, the way ice moves at the edge of things before you notice. He felt the bond, I realized. The curse had been screaming over it for five days; now it was clear, and Glacius could read its frequency the way all high-level practitioners could.

He looked away.

"Valentina's patience is not infinite," he said. "Shard has moved three companies north. She will want you on the field within the fortnight."

"I'll be there," I said. "When I'm ready."

He absorbed this without argument. Then, quieter: "Why choose it? The bond." Not an accusation. A question he was not quite asking about me.

"Because what's on the other side of the inconvenience is worth every complication," I said.

The frost settled thicker around his boots. He said nothing, and his silence had a particular quality.

"She'll bring warmth," I said. "Your Shadow Twin." He went very still. I held his gaze. "When you find her. It is a welcome feeling, Glacius. More than I had words for."

He said nothing. Then he pushed off the wall and was gone, through the frost, without ceremony, the pavement where he'd stood fractionally colder than the rest.

I went back inside.

She was waking up.

Not quietly. The transition came in from all directions at once: sound, scent, sensation, the weight of everything. She took it the way she'd taken everything unfamiliar for the past week: spine rigid, jaw set, hands finding whatever was nearest. Which was mine.

She could grip considerably harder than she used to.

The first day was the worst. The awakening was violent by design, the virus taking hold, every system slamming up to speed. She ran hot. Not fever in the human sense; this heat came from inside the tissue, from the cellular rebuild happening beneath the skin. Her grip went crushing-tight, then slack, then tight again as she surfaced and submerged in waves.

I offered my wrist the first time shortly after midnight. The blood helped anchor the process, a medical fact I had explained beforehand and a reality I was not prepared for, which was: the bond going slightly warmer in the dark, her hold on my wrist certain even half-unconscious, the same precision she applied to everything translating into this without effort.

She only ever took what she needed. Even through the worst of it. That was also entirely her.

I stayed. I talked. For three days I talked more continuously than I had in five centuries of conscious existence, because silence made the disorientation worse and my voice was something she could locate when everything else was coming in too fast. I talked about the salt circle geometry she'd declared structurally unsound before watching me draw a perfect one in three seconds. About the terrible coffee. About the plant I'd killed in the corner on Day One that was still sitting in its windowsill pot as a cautionary exhibit. About the croissants neither of us had finished.

I gave her my blood again on the second day, when the fever spiked highest and the bond went thin in a way I recognized as pain. And again on the third, when it began to ease, the heat pulling back like a tide retreating, her grip loosening degree by degree into something that felt less like survival and more like rest.

On the morning of the fourth day, she went still.

Not the death-still of the first night. This was different. Quieter. Complete.

One breath. Two.

When she opened her eyes, they were violet.

Not her color, not the analytical silver she'd arrived with, the aura-reader's steady gray. The deep, clear violet of Nyx warrior lineage.

She blinked. Looked at the ceiling. At me. Then, with the deliberateness of a woman conducting an inventory, around the basement.

"I've been thinking," she said, voice rough and gaining ground with each word, "about the velvet curtains."

I stared at her.

"When we leave here." She pushed herself up on one elbow, entirely unhurried for a woman who had just survived conversion. "We are not going back to Early Century Dungeon chic. I want that on record, upfront, before you have time to become attached to the aesthetic."

"They block the sun," I said.

It was the same defense I had given when she had seen my apartment in a bond-vision and spent ten minutes cataloguing everything wrong with it.

"IKEA," she said. "First week. Non-negotiable. I have been planning our route through the showroom for approximately four days and I will not be dissuaded by a man who describes velvet curtains as practical."

The laugh came out without warning. Full and unguarded and entirely undignified, the kind that arrives without permission and departs the same way, and I did not try to stop it. It had too much behind it: five days of dying and not dying, forty-five minutes of pillow rearrangement, and this woman opening her eyes violet and immediately resuming an argument she had started three days ago in someone else's apartment.

I kissed her. Brief and certain, the kind that didn't need to announce itself, because everything that needed to be said had already been said in the laugh.

When I pulled back, her violet eyes were warm in the way I was still learning to receive without bracing for it to stop.

"You'll need to feed," I said. Not a question. I turned my wrist and offered it, the same instinct as handing her something she needed before she'd fully registered the need herself.

She looked at my wrist. Then at me. "You're very calm about this."

"You are not the first new vampire I have managed," I said. "You are, however, the only one I intended to keep."

She took my wrist. The first drink was careful, then not. After a moment she pulled back, her eyes brighter than before, and regarded me with the slightly recalibrated expression of someone updating a prior model.

"Hm," she said.

"Hm," I agreed.

I reached out and tucked a strand of silver-blonde hair back from her face. Her violet eyes tracked the movement and came back to mine.

"Welcome," I said, "to the rest of it."

She settled against my side, warm, solid, entirely real, and looked up at me.

"First week," she said. "Curtains down."

"First week," I agreed.

Chapter 8: Marked Forever

Six months later, I was still occasionally surprised by what I could do.

Not in a look-at-me-I'm-a-vampire way, mostly in a practical, this-is-actually-useful sort of way. The aura readings were sharper now, which made my job significantly more efficient. My sense of smell had become a liability in certain parts of the city and an asset in most others. I could draw a warding circle in the dark, by touch, in about twelve seconds, which Cassius had timed and found acceptable.

The coffee still tasted wrong. Vampire senses, it turned out, were extremely good at detecting every single thing that made cheap safe house coffee undrinkable, and six months in I had not yet made peace with this development.

The velvet curtains were still up. This was an ongoing negotiation. I was winning, but it was taking longer than planned, because Cassius negotiated the way he did everything: with infinite patience and the unshakable conviction that he was right. He was not right. He would eventually accept this.

In the meantime, we were putting on formal black tie and going to my own bonding ceremony, which was a sentence I could not have constructed in any reality a year ago.

The bonding ceremony was at Velvet Shadow. Draven Emeris's club, which sat over his vault and smelled of old money and aged stone. Cyprian Valen officiated. Of course he did. He brought his tablet.

The ceremony was brief and formal, which suited both of us. Cassius handled the vows with the focused efficiency of a man reading a tactical briefing. His voice didn't waver. Mine didn't either. I had decided in advance that if I was going to say *my life is yours* in public, I was going to say it like I meant it and move on we had already said it in more difficult circumstances and the meaning hadn't changed.

What changed: at the end, when Cyprian made his official notation and the Council documentation was completed, a new mark appeared on my wrist. Small, clean, deep violet, placed just above where the curse veins had been, as though the magic had known exactly where to put it.

Cyprian glanced at it without ceremony. "The Nyx mark. Confirms a bond that superseded a blood curse through voluntary love. There are perhaps twelve on record in six hundred years of practice." His pen clicked. "Congratulations. Try not to make my job interesting again."

Cassius looked at the mark for a long time. When he said something, it was: "It suits you."

Which was Cassius for *you are extraordinary.* I had learned to translate.

The reception at Velvet Shadow involved champagne I could actually taste now - sharper, cleaner, changed. A crowd of supernaturals in formal black, and Sloane Caffrey finding me in the first three minutes and immediately having opinions about the tattoo.

"It's *beautiful*," she said, grabbing my wrist and turning it over with the enthusiasm of someone who had been doing this for a year and had not yet run out of strong feelings. "The violet matches your eyes. Did you plan that?"

"I did not plan any of this," I said, which was technically true and somehow also summarized everything.

Draven materialized behind Sloane like an architectural wall in a suit. He nodded at me once. This was, apparently, approval.

Kael Nightshade appeared with Maya beside him, she was already smiling before she reached me. She had been through her own version of this the year before. Her expression was the expression of someone who knew exactly what the other person just survived.

"You made it," she said.

"Barely," I said.

"That's how it goes," she said. We left it at that, because it was also enough.

I found Glacius at the edge of the room, standing near a pillar with the posture of a man who had agreed to attend and was committed to regretting it. The frost hadn't followed him inside, he was controlled enough for that, but the air near him was four degrees colder than it should have been.

"You've been standing there for forty minutes," I said. "There's a perfectly good open bar."

"I don't drink," he said.

"And yet you came."

"Cassius invited me." As though this were a natural force, not a decision.

I looked at him, at the careful, complete stillness he used like armor. "I know what it feels like," I said. "Thinking that not choosing something is safer than choosing wrong."

He said nothing.

"It's not," I said. "It's just slower." I picked up my champagne. "You don't have to believe me. But you asked Cassius why he'd choose the inconvenience." I met his ice-blue gaze. "You're still asking."

I left him with that, because I wasn't making an argument. Cassius was beside me before I'd taken three steps.

"You can't fix him," he said.

"I wasn't trying to fix him," I said. "I was giving profound relationship insight to someone who was accidentally air-conditioning the venue."

He considered this. "It might help."

"It might," I agreed. "Or it gives him something to be cold and silent about for the next several months. Either way, he showed up."

The loft was quiet when we got home.

We had been working on it, that was the word we used, which meant some furniture had been replaced, the artwork was in negotiation, and Cassius still occasionally woke at dawn out of reflex and then remembered there was no operational reason he had to. The velvet curtains were still in the bedroom window. Last front of a long campaign.

I stood in the kitchen and made tea. He sat on the still-slightly-terrible plaid sofa and watched me, because at some point he had decided that watching me make tea was a thing worth doing, and I had given up commenting on it.

"Your toast was very short," he said.

"It was a toast, not a summary document. Did it say what it needed to say?"

A pause. "Yes."

"Then it was the right length."

I brought the tea over and sat beside him. He reached for my wrist, the way he did now, automatically, a touch that had stopped needing permission, and his thumb traced the new violet mark. Lightly. Careful in the way he was always careful with things that mattered.

"Still suits you," he said.

It was a fine life. Inconvenient in specific ways, complicated in ways I hadn't anticipated, not at all what I had planned.

"The curtains," I said.

"Are staying," he said, but the corner of his mouth moved.

"They are not."

"We'll discuss it."

"We are discussing it. Right now."

He turned and looked at me with the full patient weight of a man who had stood at Lepanto and survived the Salem incident and was fairly certain he could outlast a curtain argument.

"Not tonight," he said.

"Not tonight," I agreed.

I noted, in the privacy of my own head, that he had somehow just won this round, despite the fact that I was the one who brought it up.

GLACIUS

The sculpture garden was a bad place to be in a blizzard. Glacius Diamante had been in worse.

He crossed the frozen grounds in fifteen seconds, moving through frost rather than over it, and stopped at the center of the garden where his tracking sense said the breach had occurred. He took in the scene in a single sweep: a rogue faction operative, the insignia of Konstantin Shard's breakaway cell visible on the collar, third confirmed rebel contact in two weeks, which was no longer a pattern and had become a problem, and a human witness who was not going to be given the opportunity to become a further complication.

He was six seconds too late to prevent that particular piece of paperwork.

He arrived in time for the woman who had heard.

She was crouched behind an ice sculpture of an oversized spoon, which apparently counted as art in this city – with a camera raised and the specific stillness of someone who had understood, perhaps three seconds ago, that she had made a very serious mistake in coming closer. The rogue was watching her. Glacius stepped out of the frost.

The fight was brief. Rogues of this caliber did not survive engagements with Frost Wardens. He handled it with the economy of someone for whom this was administrative, noted the Shard insignia again for his report, and filed it under *escalating.*

Then the woman stood up from behind the spoon.

In five hundred and thirty-four years: two combat tours, three centuries of enforcement work. One execrable evening in Minneapolis spent at a bonding ceremony he had been socially obligated to attend. Glacius Diamante had never stopped moving because of someone's *scent.*

He caught hers.

He stopped.

Cassius's voice arrived in his head, as it had been doing with irritating frequency since the night outside the safe house. *She'll bring warmth. Your Shadow Twin. It is a welcome feeling, Glacius. More than I had words for.*

He had dismissed it. He had been dismissing it for six months.

He reassessed his position on that.

She still had the camera. She had not run, which was statistically improbable. She was looking at him with the expression of someone who is terrified and has decided that terror is not going to be the last thing she does. Gray eyes. Chin set. Jaw tight.

He tried the compulsion. Automatic. Standard. And then: a problem.

You will forget. Go home.

She did not forget. She did not go home. She stared at him and said, quietly and with impressive composure for someone who had just watched him neutralize a supernatural operative: "What *are* you?"

Three figures materialized from the storm at the garden's edge. Shard rebels, called by the rogue's last signal before he'd stopped being useful to anyone.

Kill the witness.

"Hold on," Glacius said. Not to the rebels.

He took her arm. She made a small, indignant sound. He noted that he noticed it. He moved through the frost, beneath it, through the frozen water table, through the cold that obeyed him completely and had for three centuries.

The blizzard cut out. The noise of the city cut out. The temperature dropped further, but differently, the cold of something ancient in place of something hostile. Gray-blue ice walls. A vaulted ceiling arching into darkness. Sealed doors.

She turned in a slow circle, taking it in. He watched her take it in. He had the distinct and unwelcome sensation that this was going to require a great deal of explaining, none of which he had currently prepared.

"I'm the Frost Warden," he said. "And you're my problem now."

She looked at the sealed doors. Then at him. Her chin lifted, not quite fear, not quite defiance.

"Ember Quinn," she said. "And I have a deadline."

Shadow Bound Mates - About The Series

WELCOME TO THE SHADOW BOUND MATES SERIES

Vampires. Fated mates. A series of books where immortal grumps meet the humans who refuse to swoon on command.

In the Nyx Universe, vampires don't sparkle—they brood, kidnap, and are hilariously bad at feelings. Each has spent centuries searching for their Shadow Twin, the one person immune to their compulsion, compatible on every level, and destined to drive them absolutely insane (in the best way).

What to expect:

- Fated mates who argue their way into forever
- Banter so sharp it could draw blood
- Protective vampires with unique magical abilities
- Spicy scenes with supernatural flair ()
- Romcom tone with genuine emotional beats
- Conversion arcs (death, rebirth, and happily immortal after)

- Found family across the series
- Guaranteed HEAs for every couple

Each book is a standalone romance featuring a different vampire House and power set, but characters weave through the series, building a world where Shadow Twins find each other, build clinics, start rebellions, and occasionally save Minneapolis from vampire civil wars.

Start with any book, fall in love with them all.

Find them all at books.vabrowning.com

www.ingramcontent.com/pod-product-compliance
Lightning Source LLC
LaVergne TN
LVHW051015080826
845145LV00009B/2641

* 9 7 8 1 9 7 1 1 0 9 0 6 0 *